P9-DNO-959

THE FLASH!

By Frank Berrios • Illustrated by Ethen Beavers

A GOLDEN BOOK • NEW YORK

Copyright © 2018 DC Comics.
DC SUPER FRIENDS and all related characters and elements
are trademarks of and © DC Comics.
WB SHIELD: ™ & © Warner Bros. Entertainment Inc.
(s18)

RHUS39643

rhcbooks.com

ISBN 978-1-5247-6858-4 (trade) — ISBN 978-1-5247-6859-1 (ebook)

Printed in the United States of America   10 9 8 7 6 5 4 3

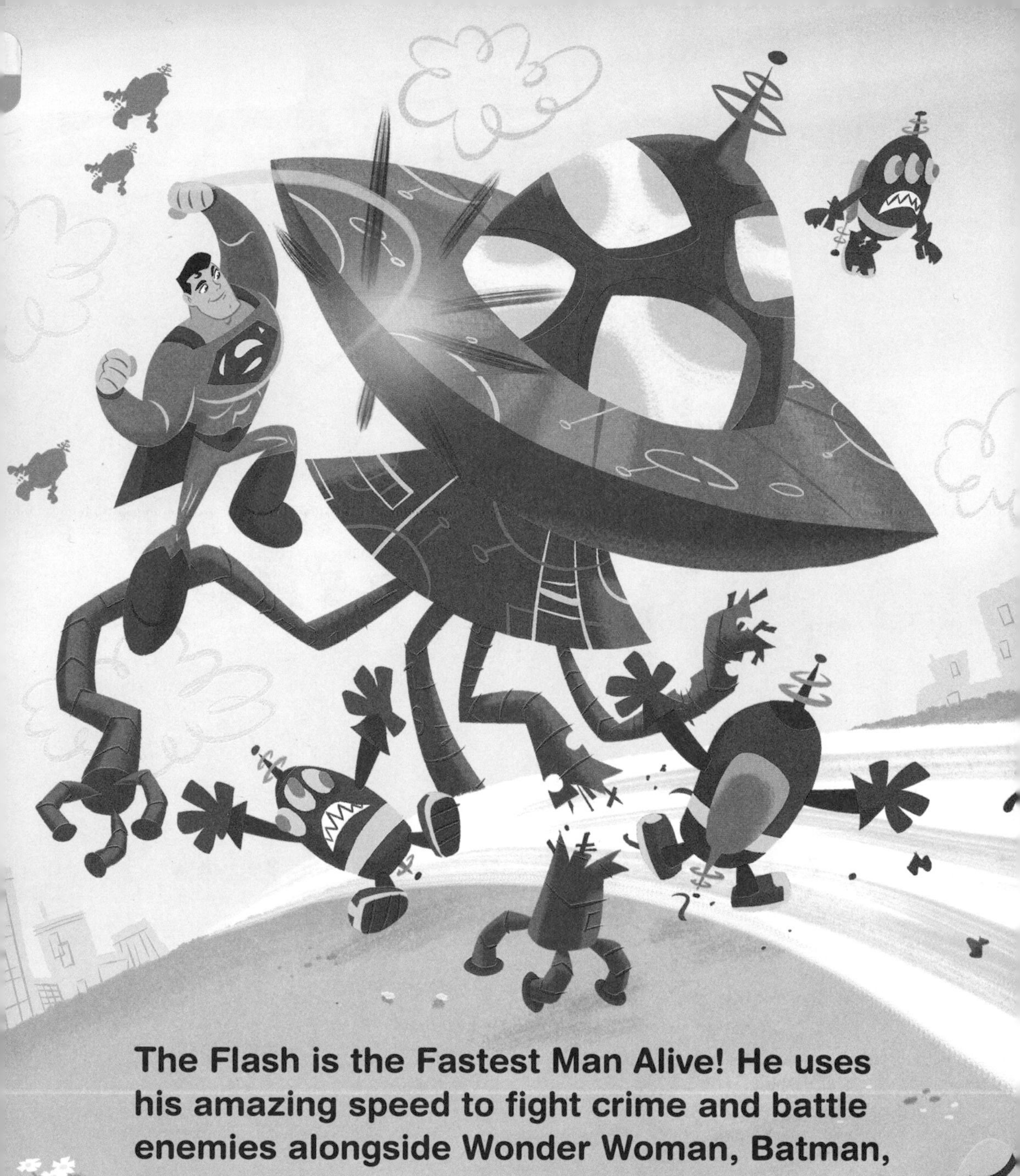

The Flash is the Fastest Man Alive! He uses his amazing speed to fight crime and battle enemies alongside Wonder Woman, Batman, Superman, and other heroes. Together they are known as the Super Friends!

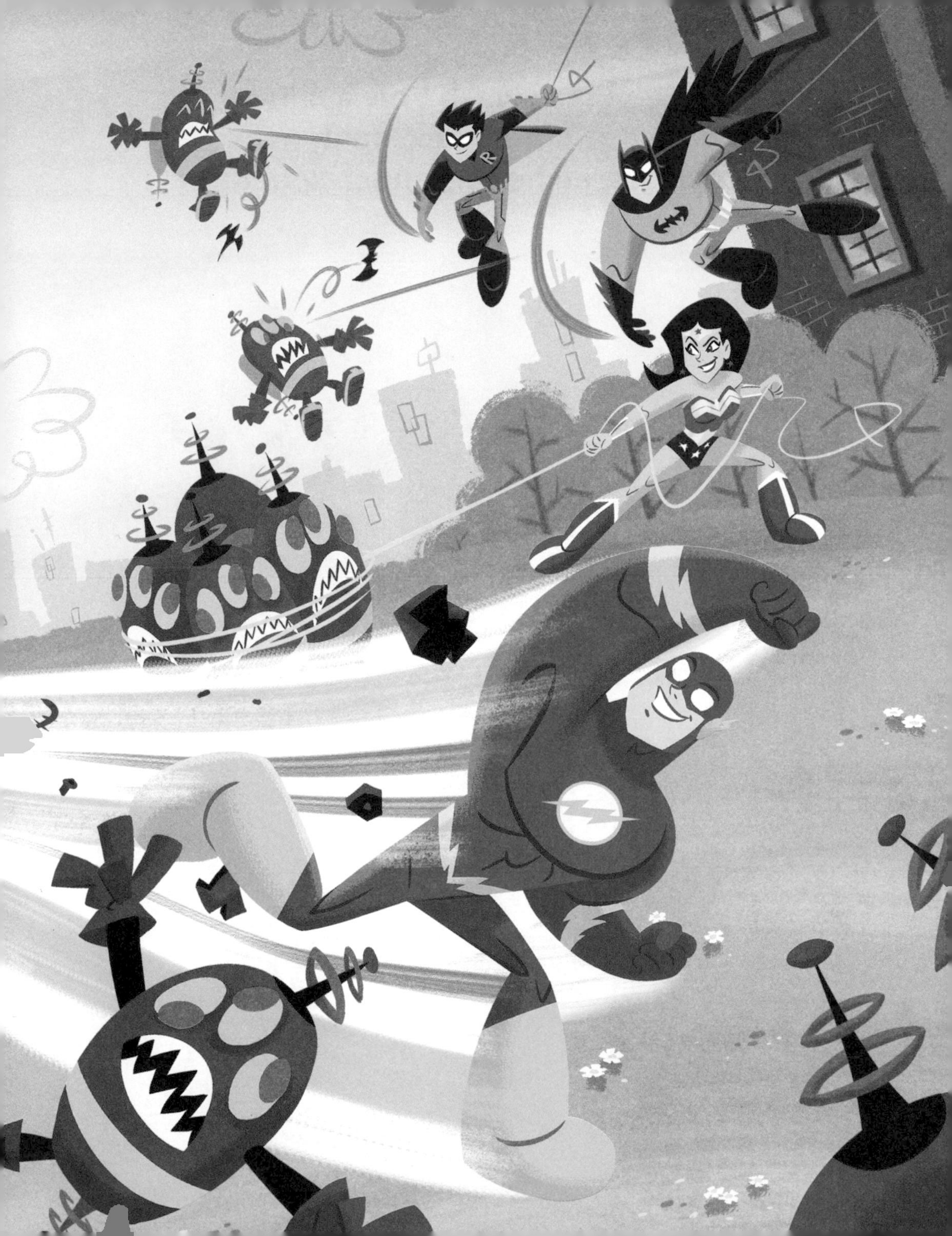

The Flash wasn't always fast. But after a freak accident, he discovered he has super-speed!

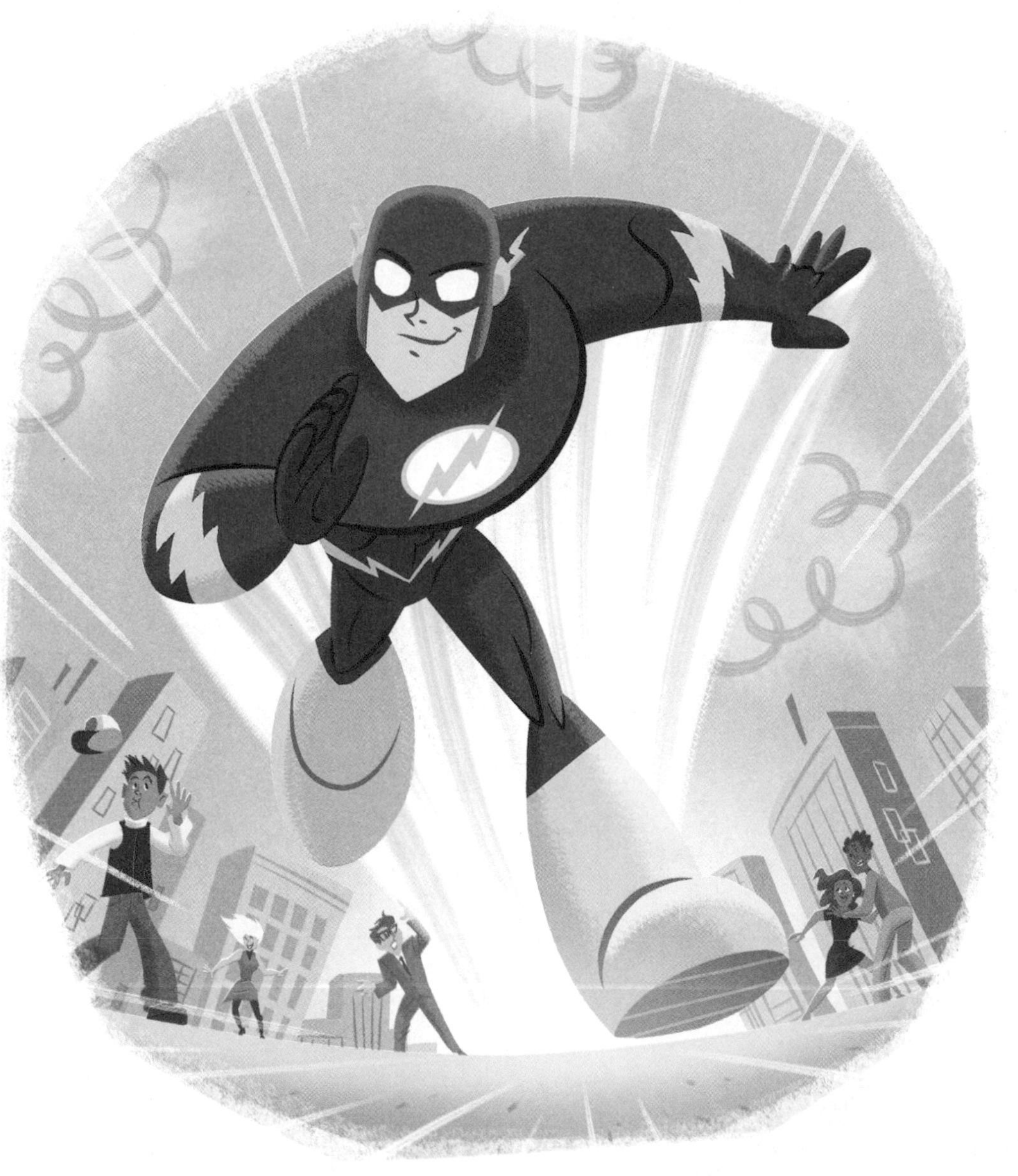

He can run faster than
the fastest race car!

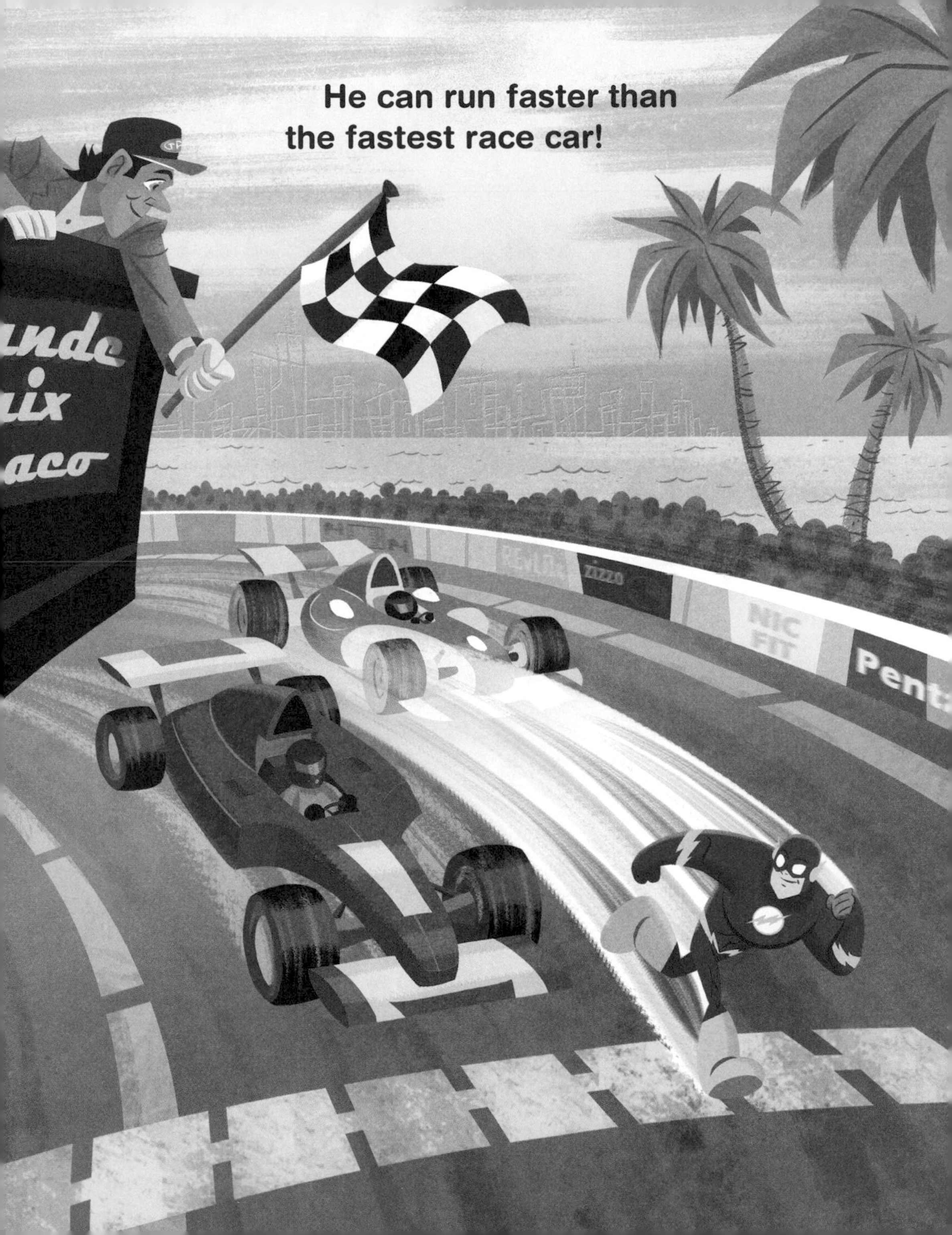
ZIZZO
NIC
FIT

He can outrun
a high-speed bullet
train!

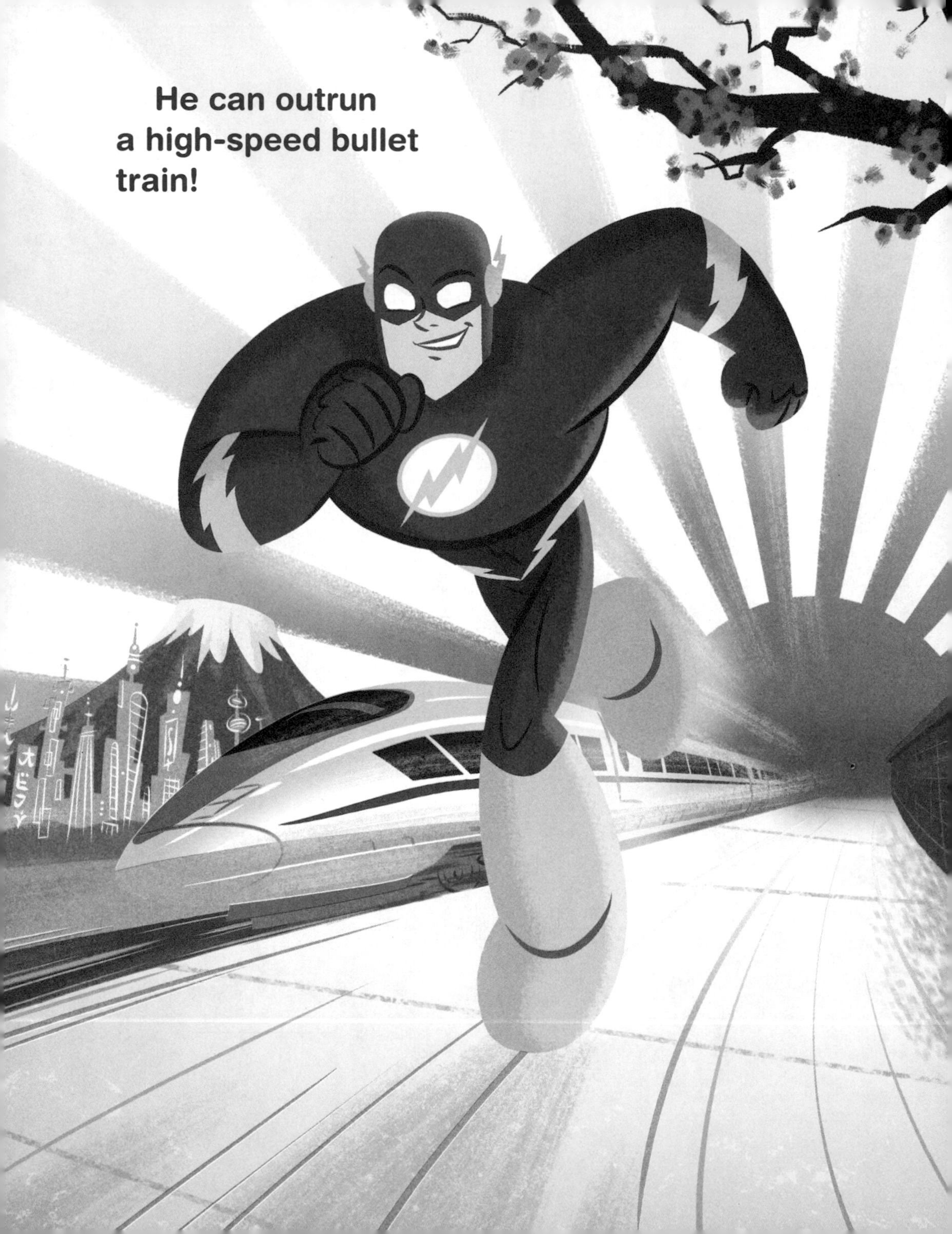

He can even run
across water—

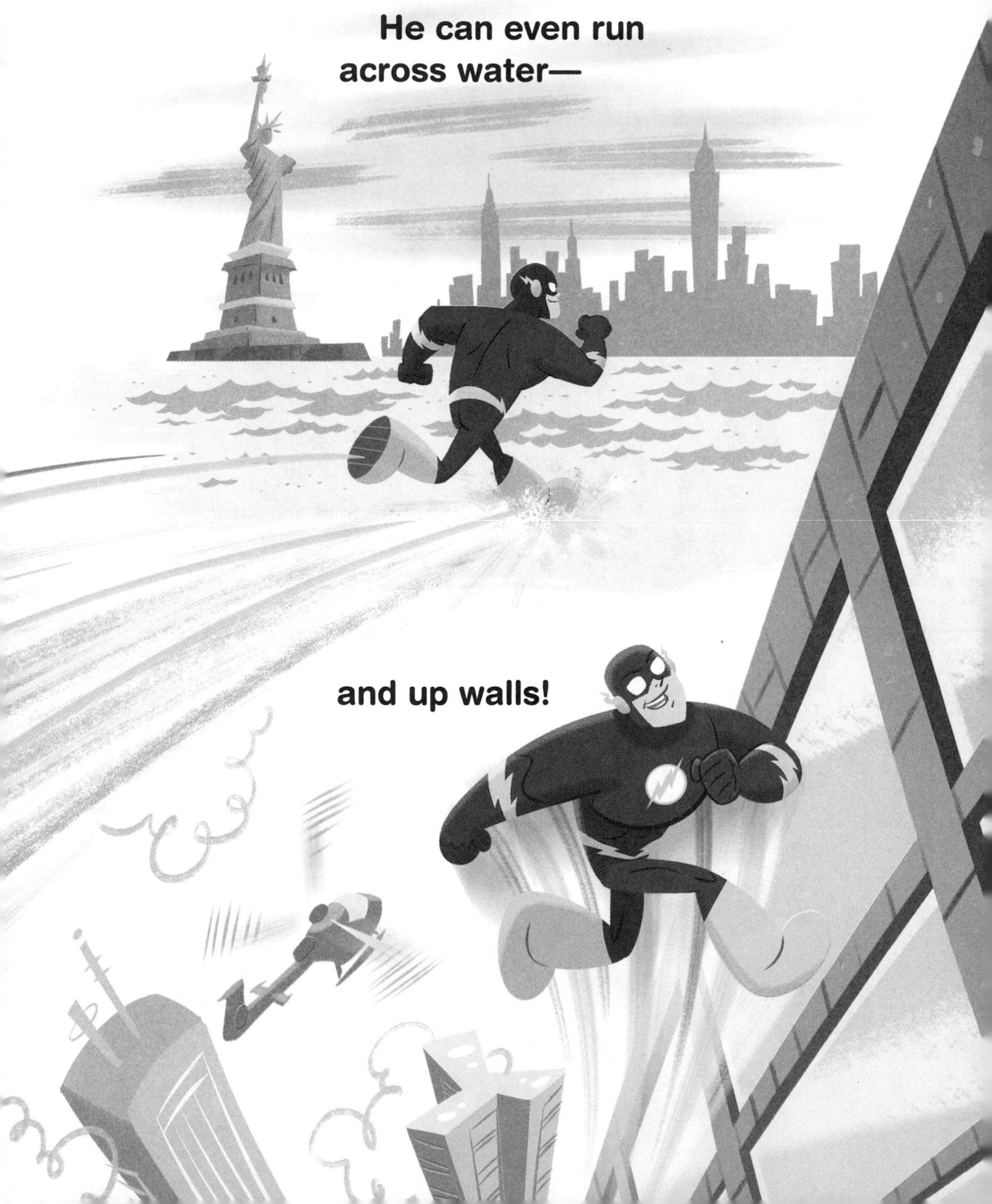

and up walls!

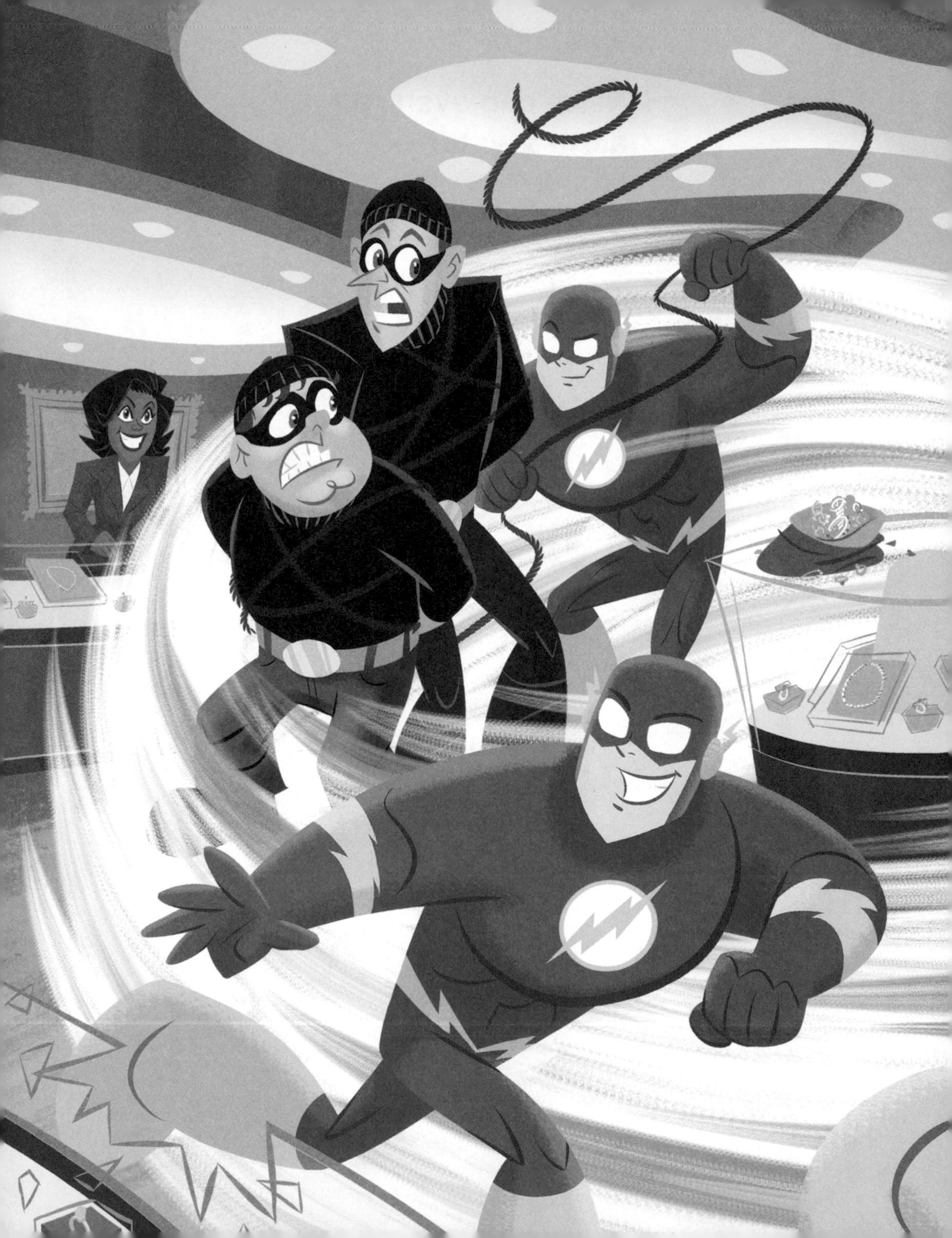

The Flash uses his power to catch criminals before they break the law. He keeps his city safe.

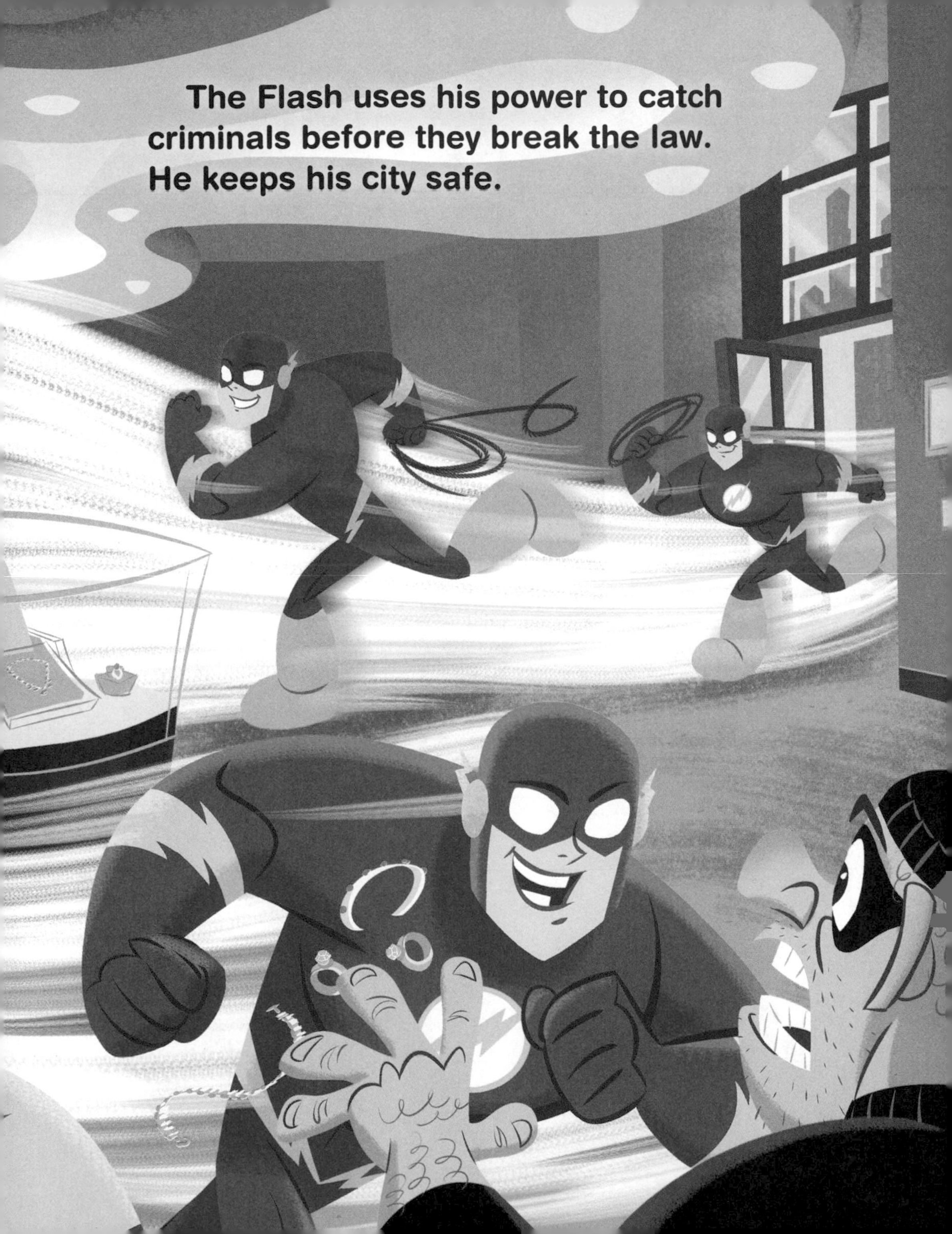

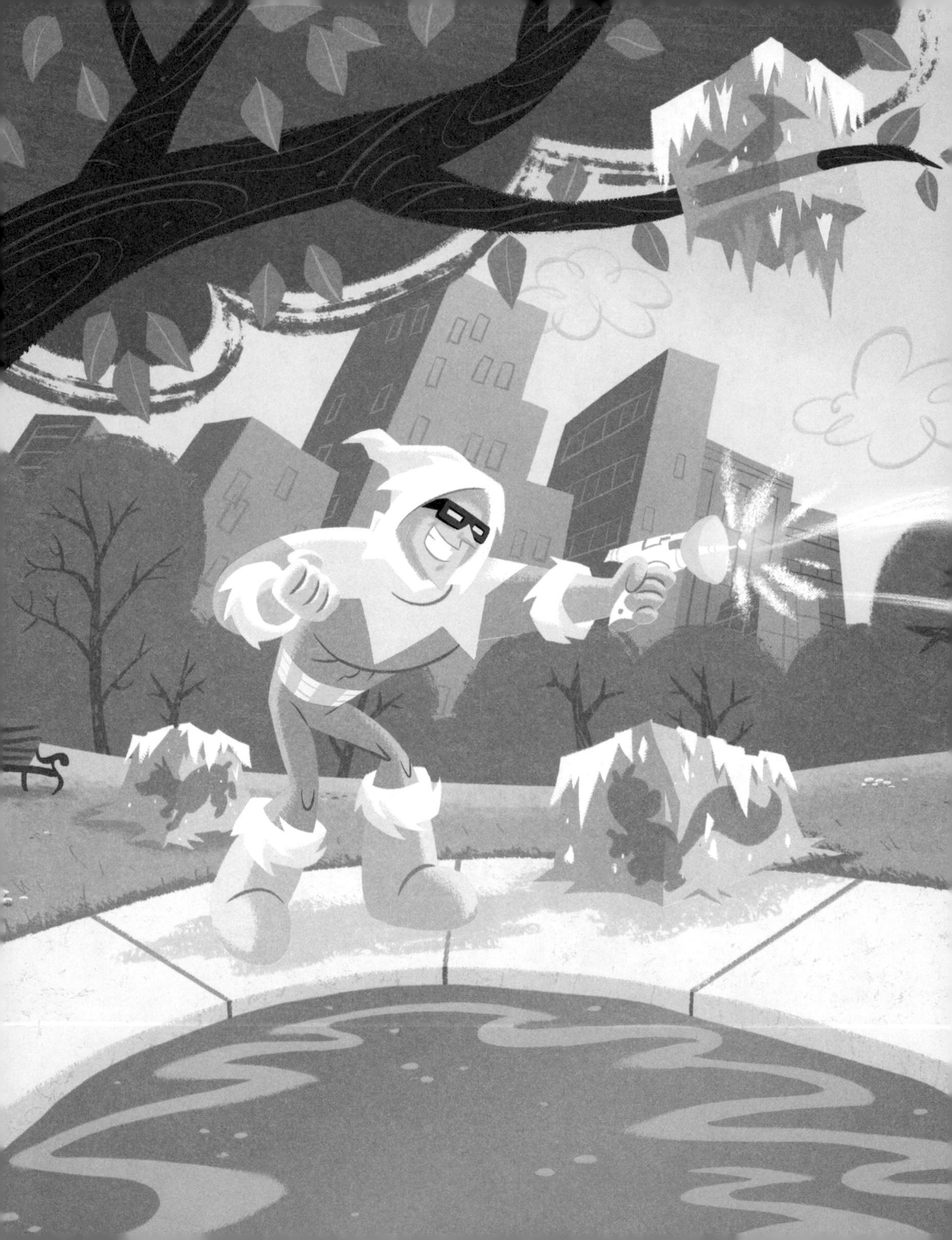

The Flash also has lots of enemies. Captain Cold is a stone-cold criminal with a cold-beam weapon that can freeze anything it hits!

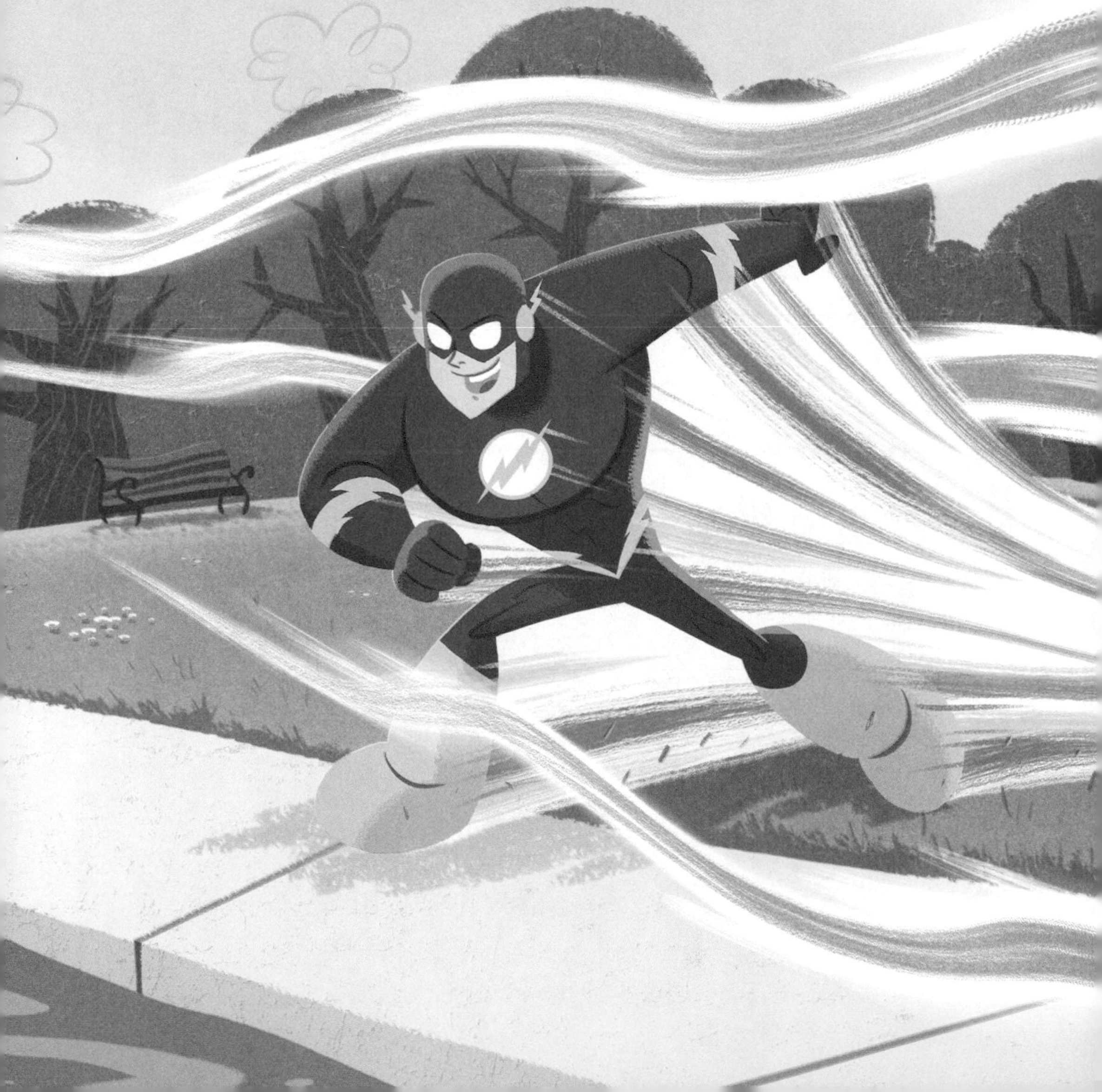

The Flash uses his super-speed to put Captain Cold on ice!

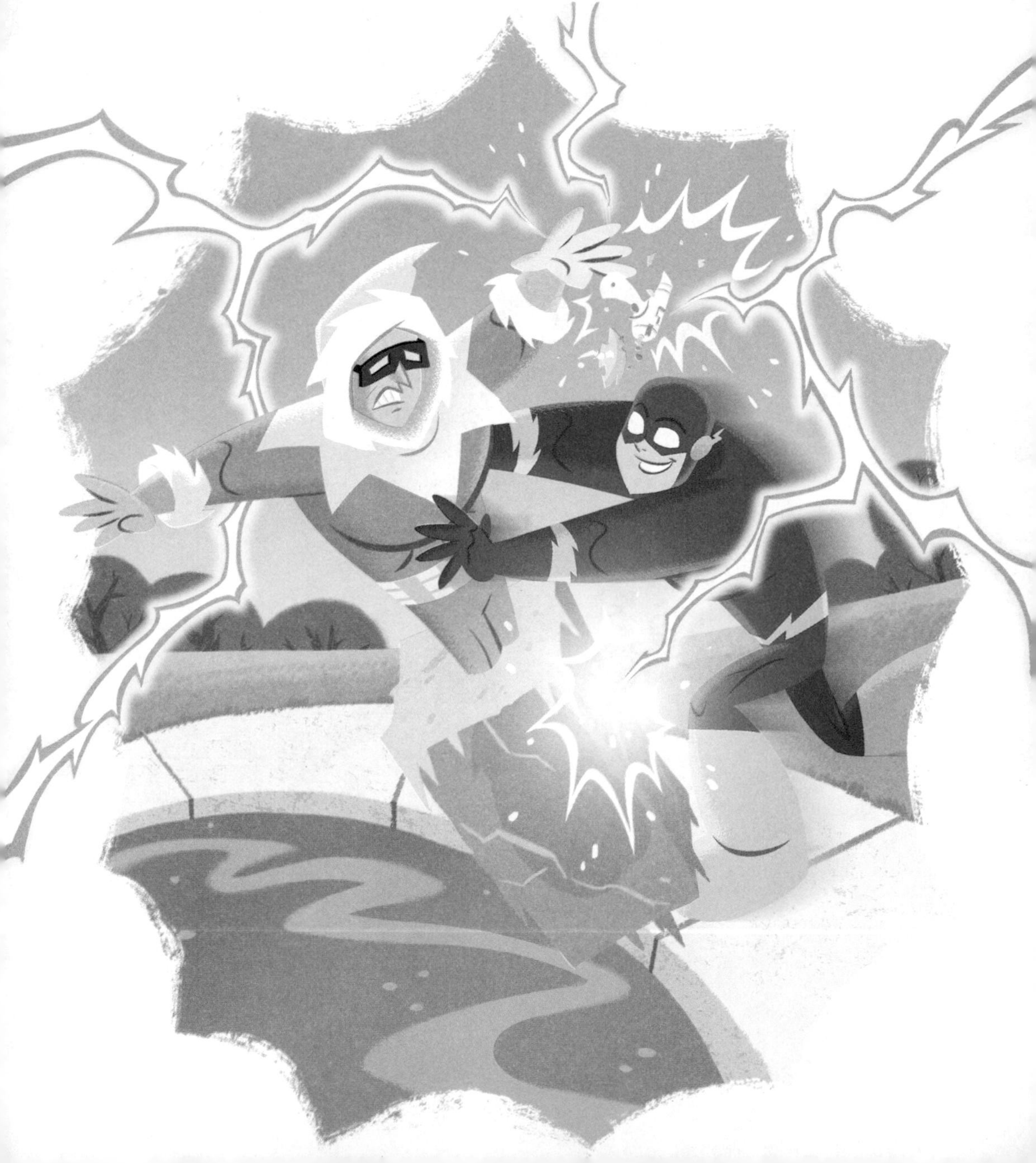

The Flash has defeated Captain Boomerang many times. But the curious criminal always comes back for more!

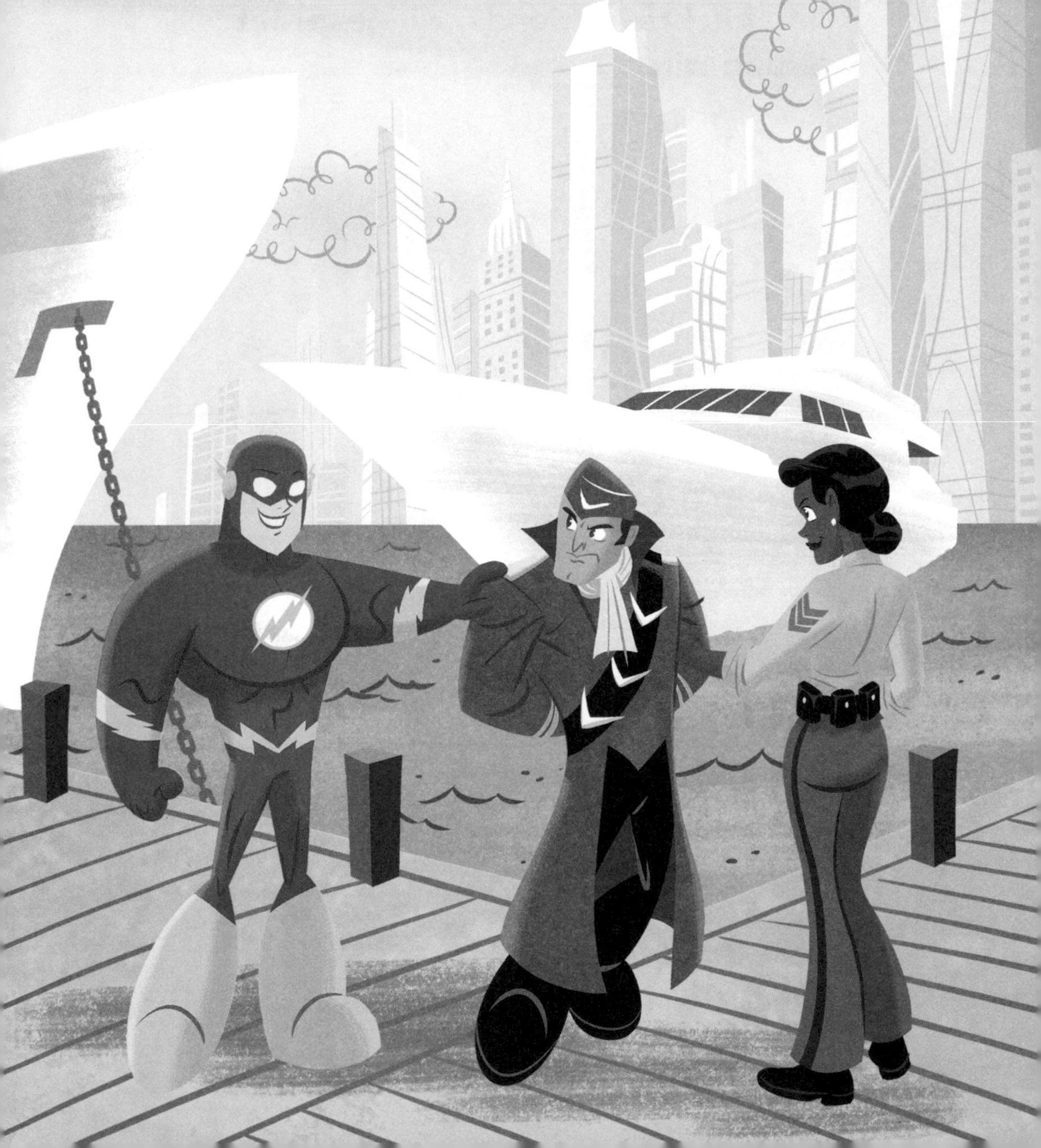

Gorilla Grodd is a super-intelligent gorilla who wants to rule the world with an army of apes. But The Flash and his brave friends will never let Grodd win!

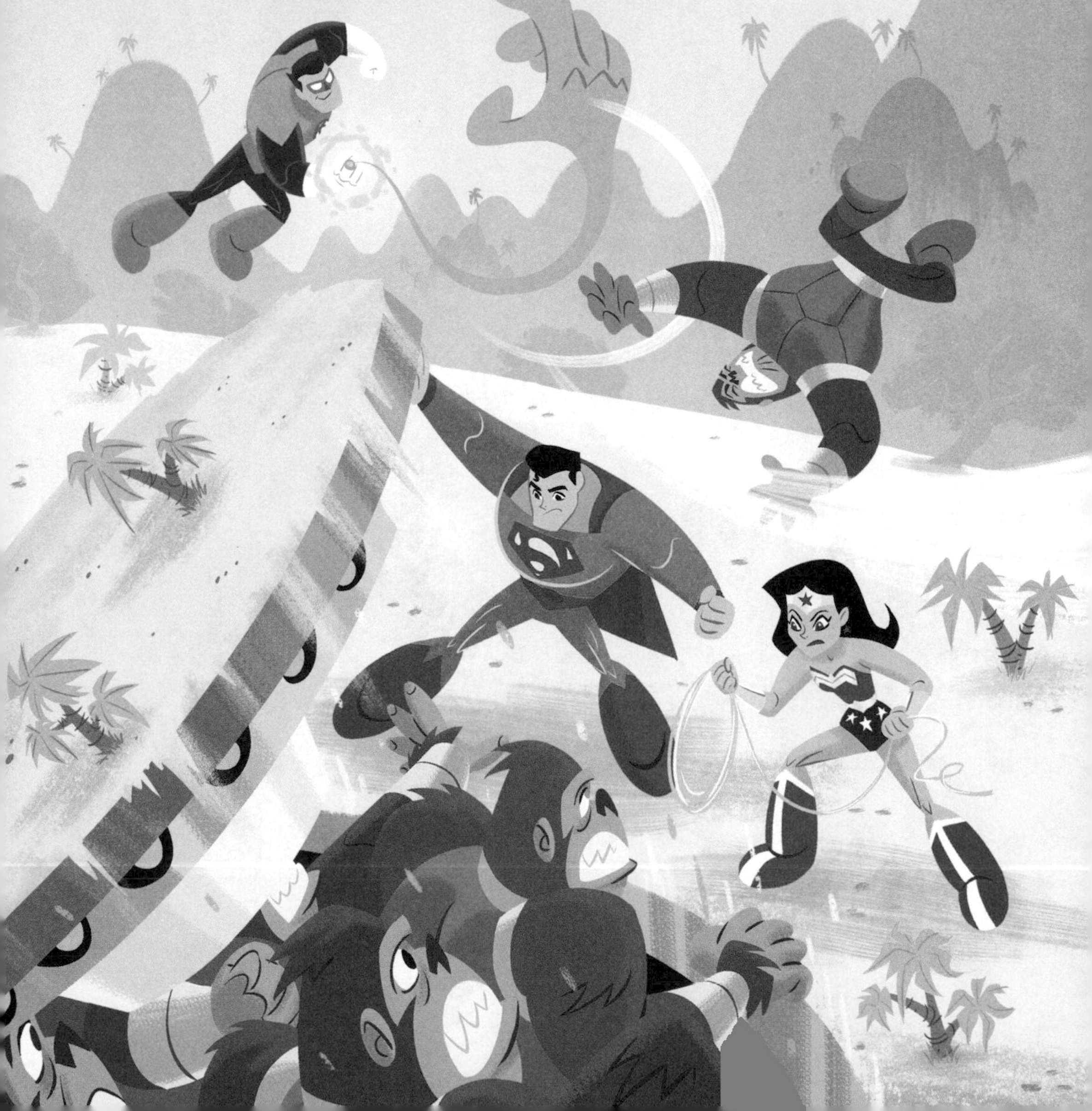

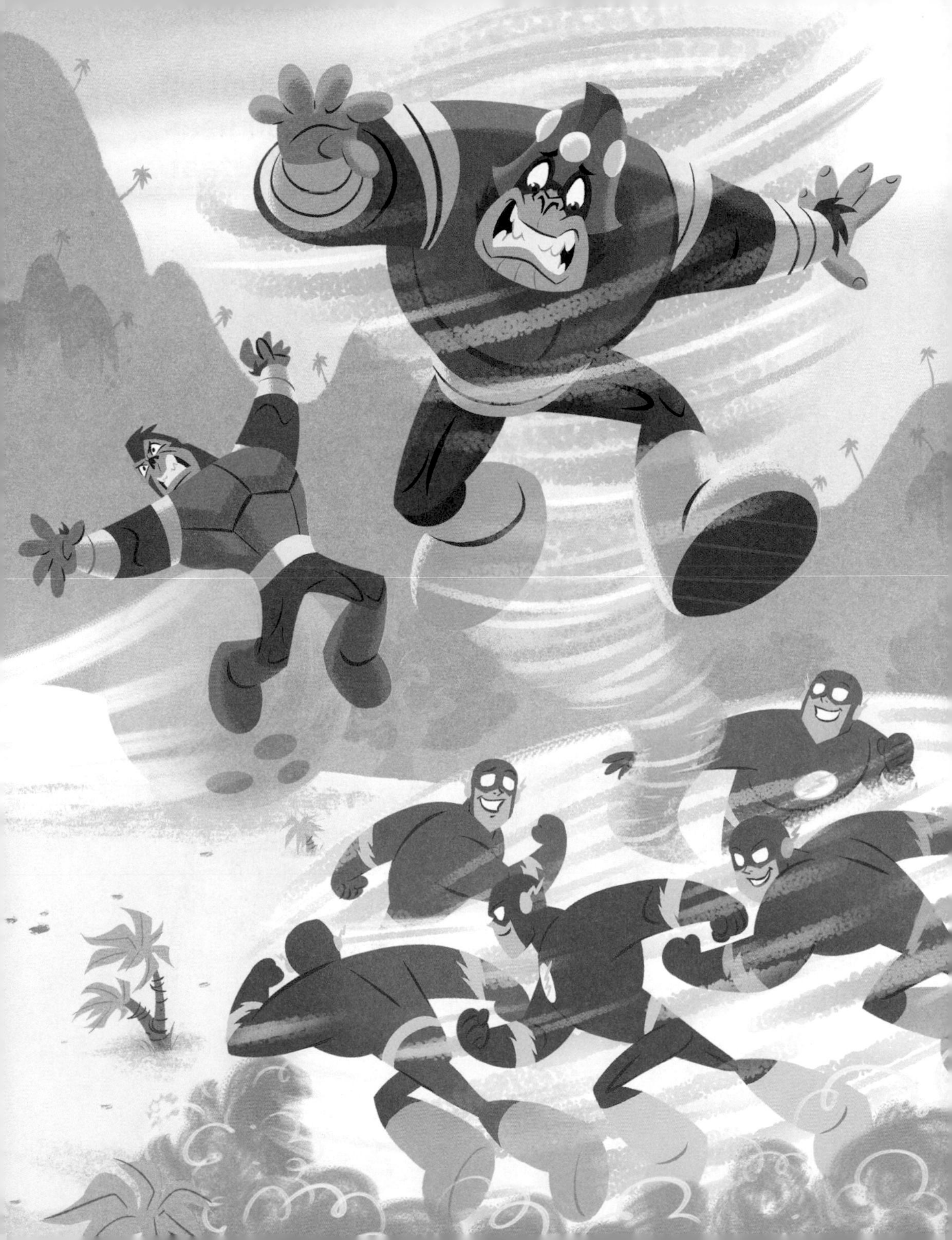

Mirror Master uses mirrors to distract and confuse his victims. The Flash uses fast moves and quick thinking to defeat this villain!

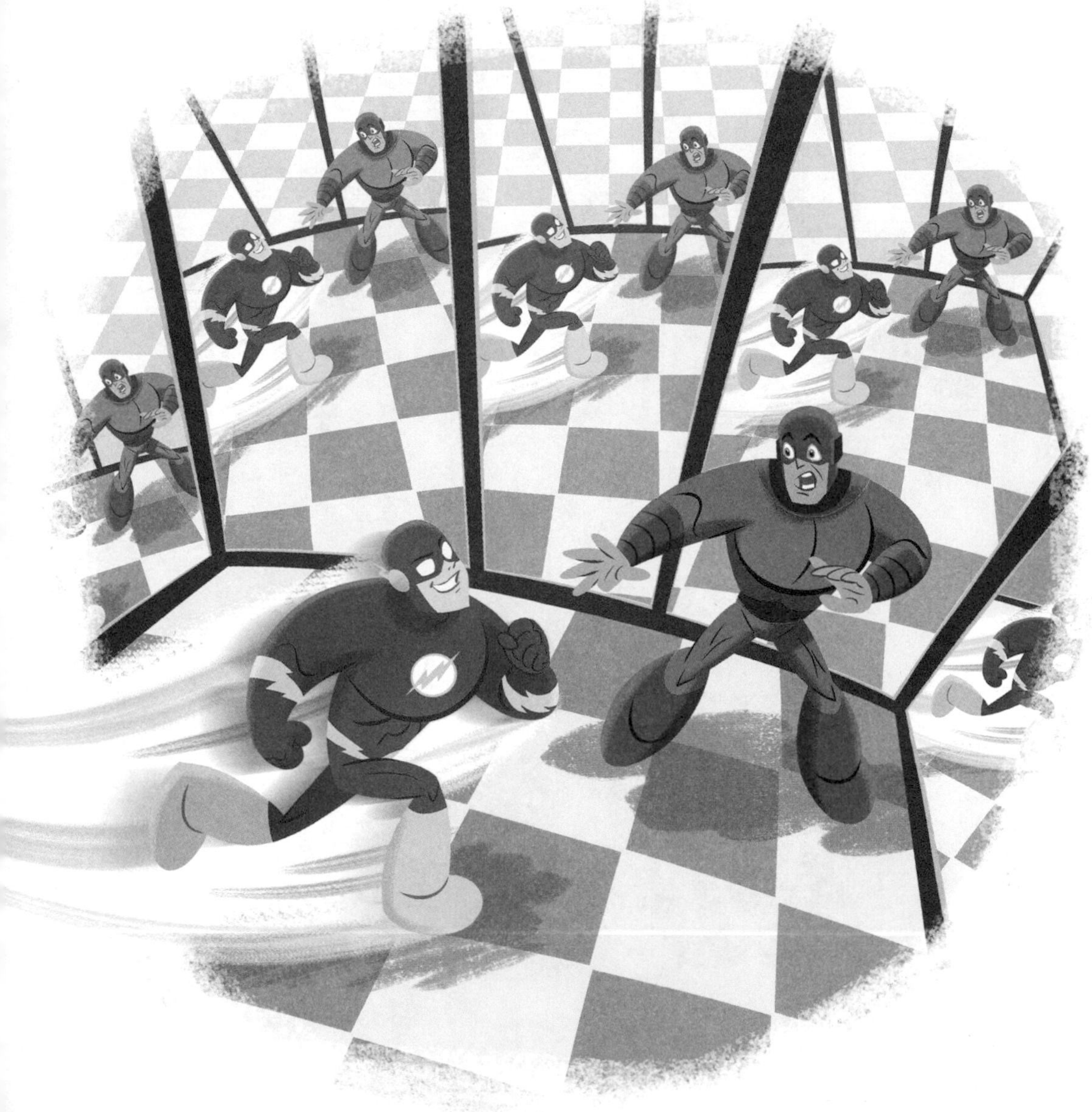

The Weather Wizard can create rain, snow, fog—and even lightning! This makes him a powerful enemy. The Flash and the Super Friends use teamwork to take him down.

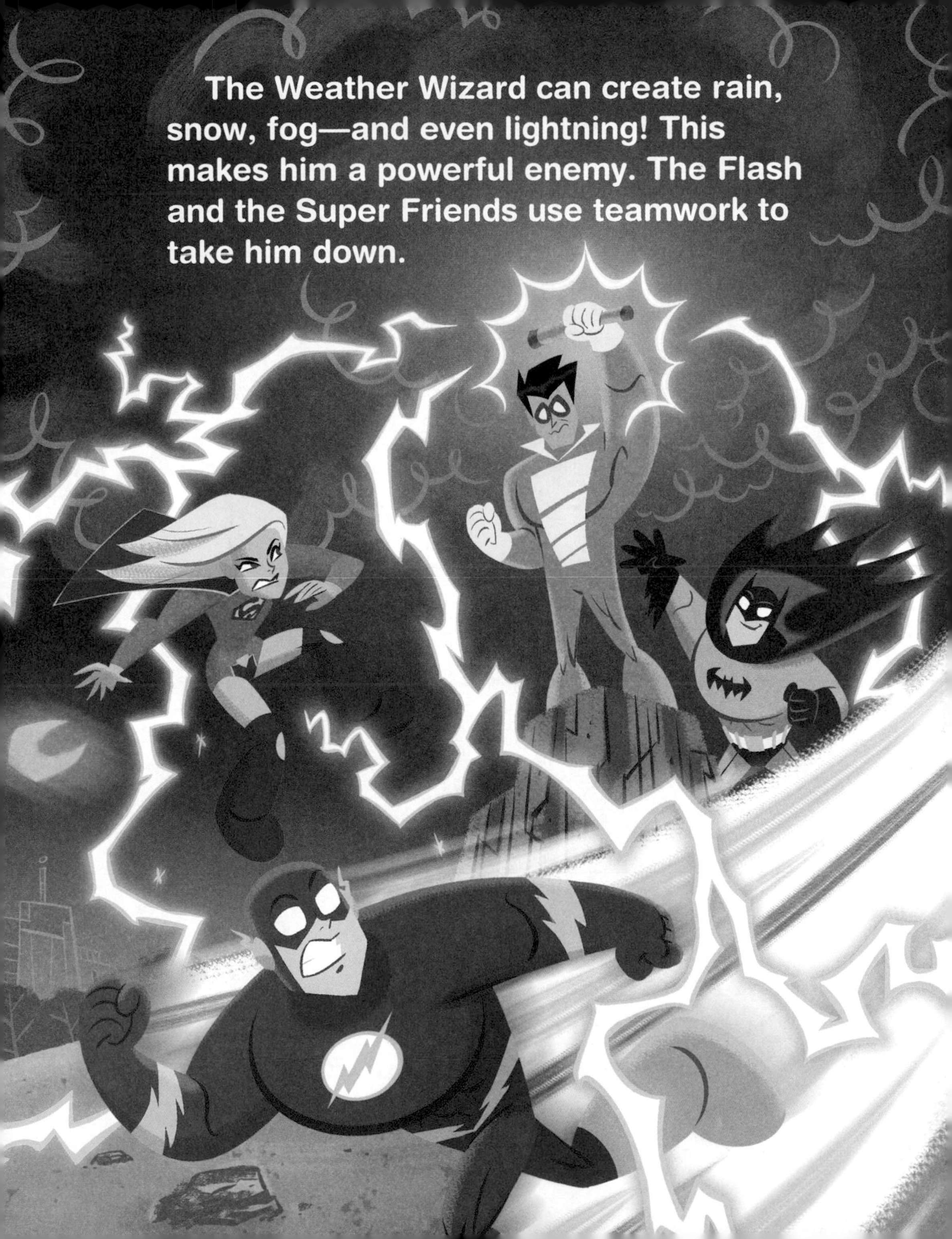

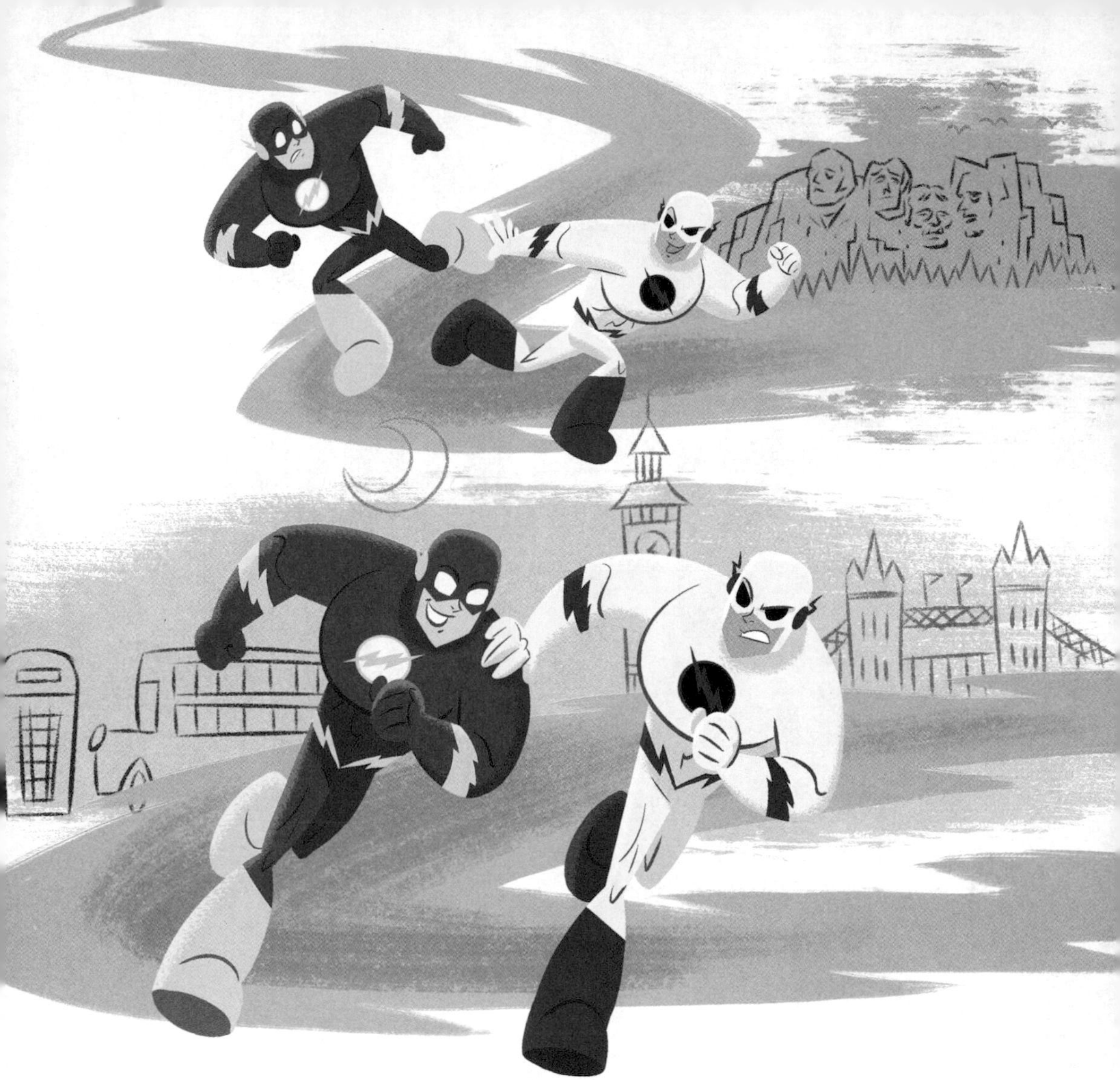

Reverse-Flash is a criminal from the future. Unlike The Flash, Reverse-Flash decided to use his super-speed to commit crimes. The Flash is ready to give this time-traveler a time-out!

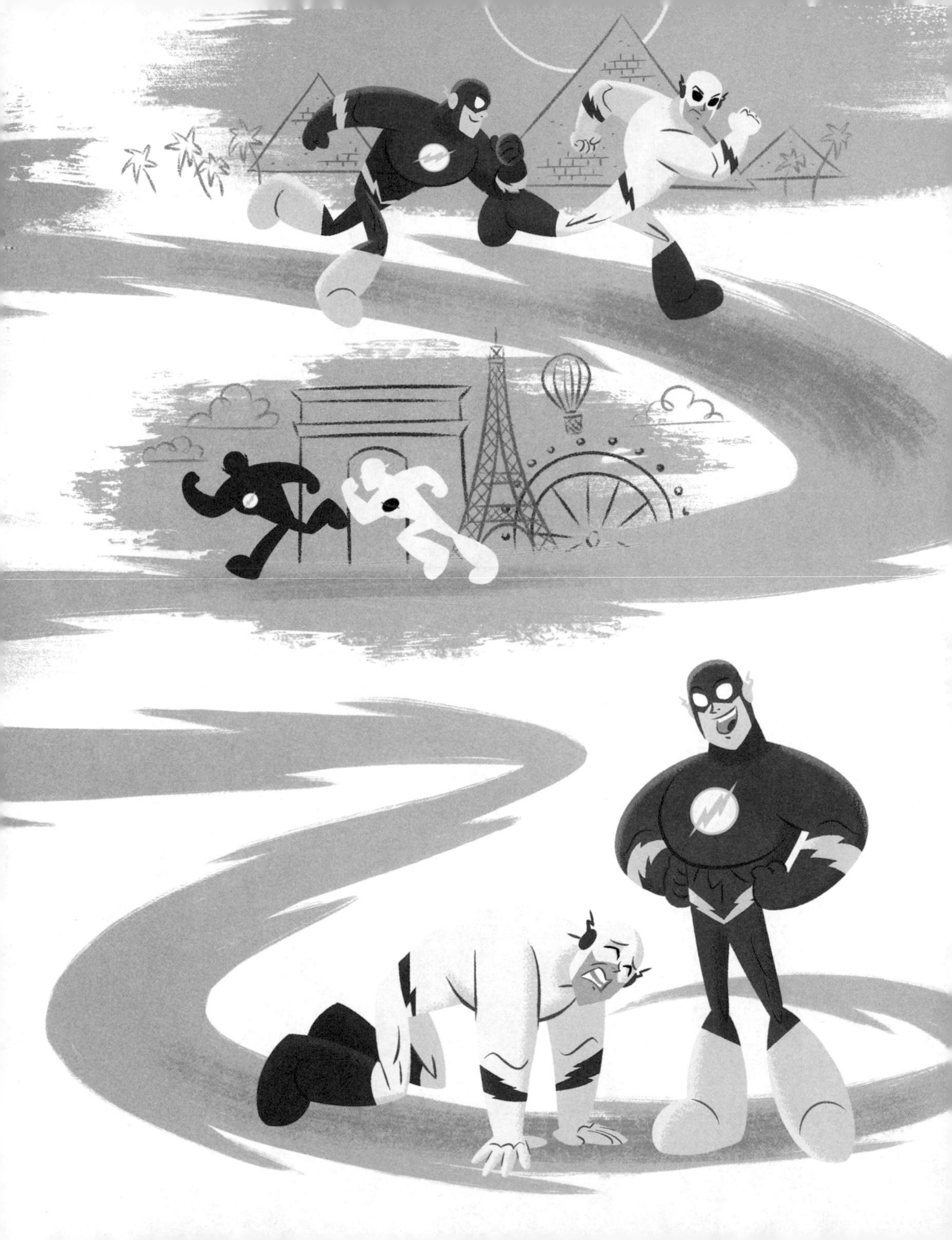

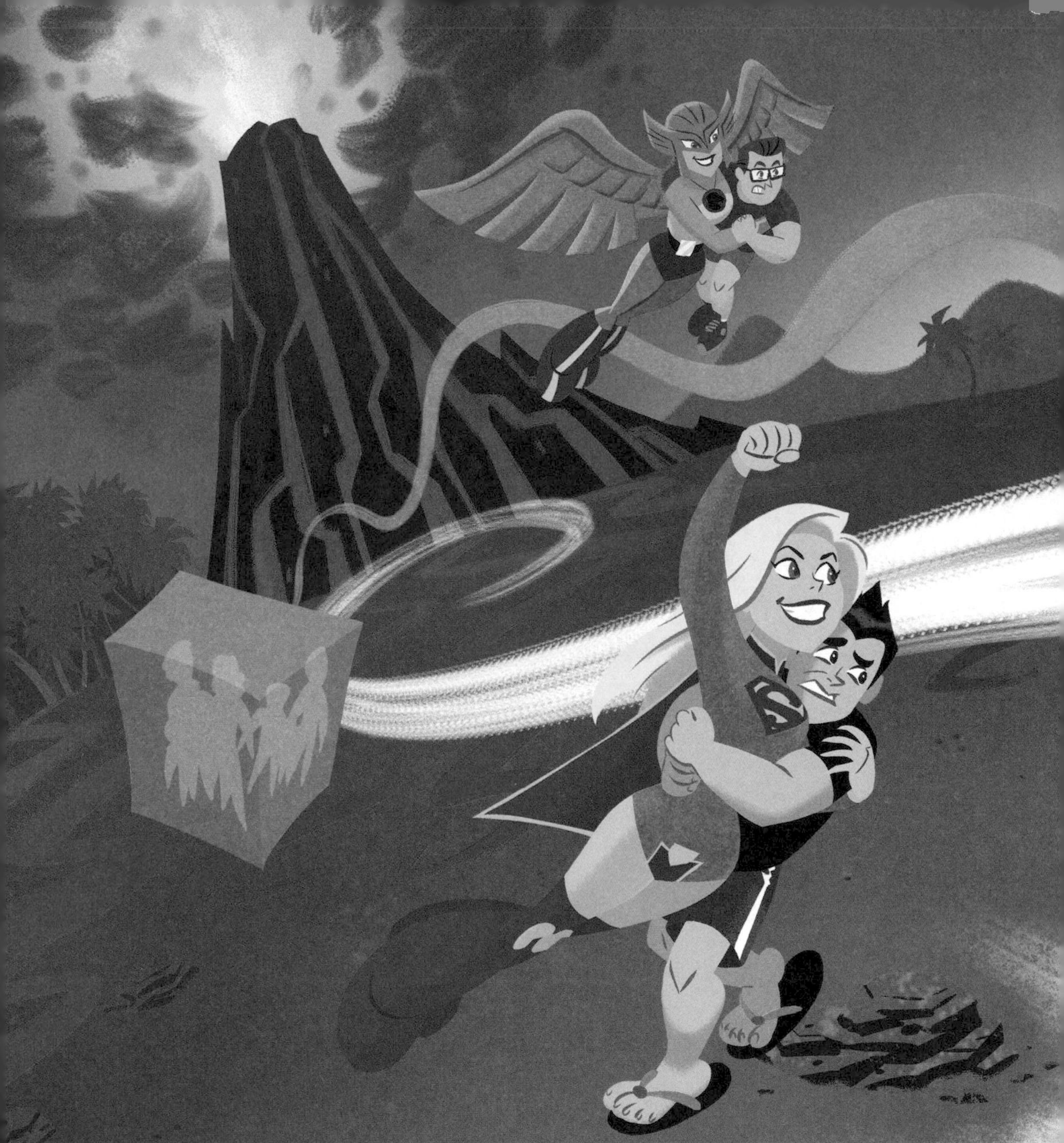

No matter the emergency, The Flash and his Super Friends are ready to race to the rescue!

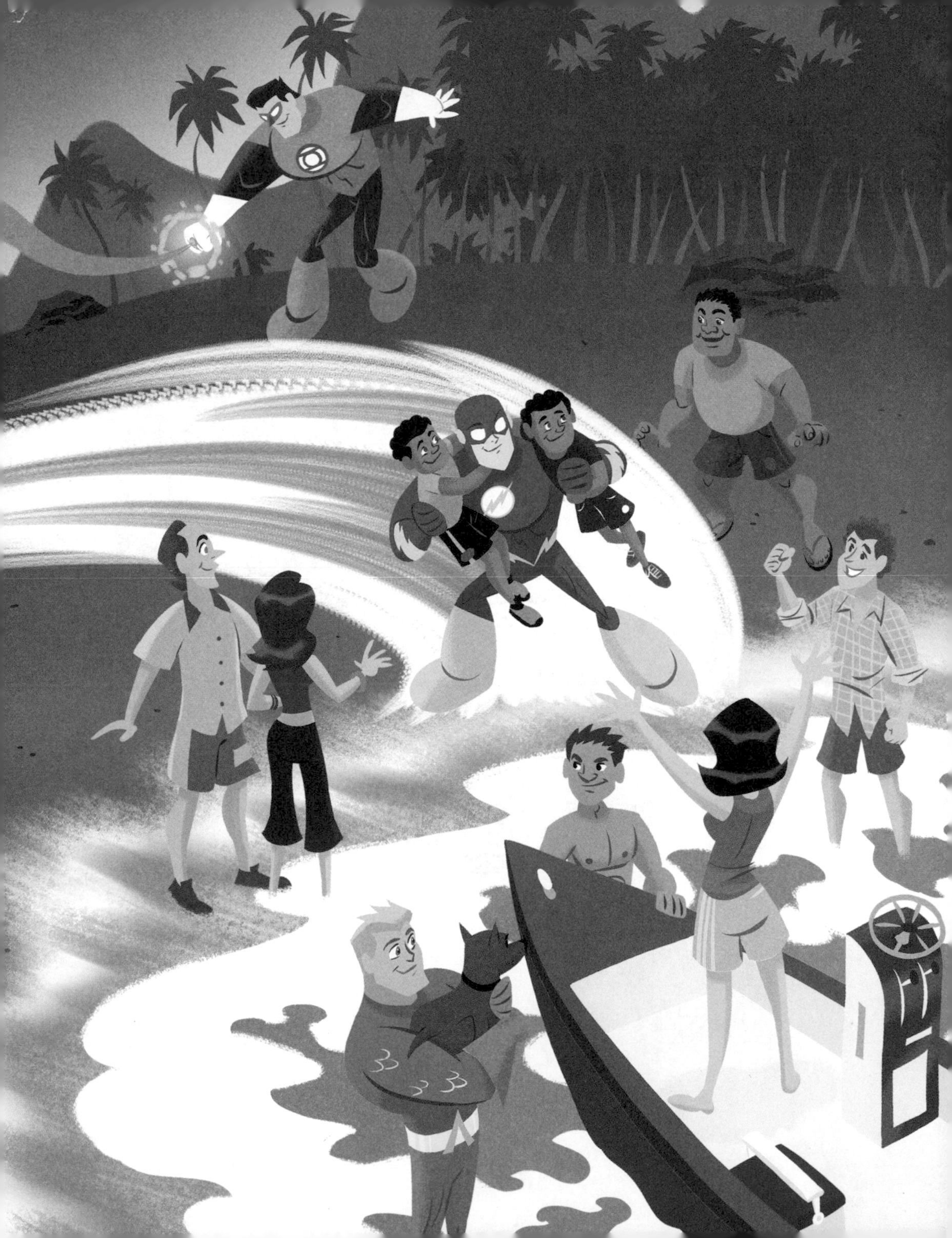

No one can run, move, or leap faster than The Flash.

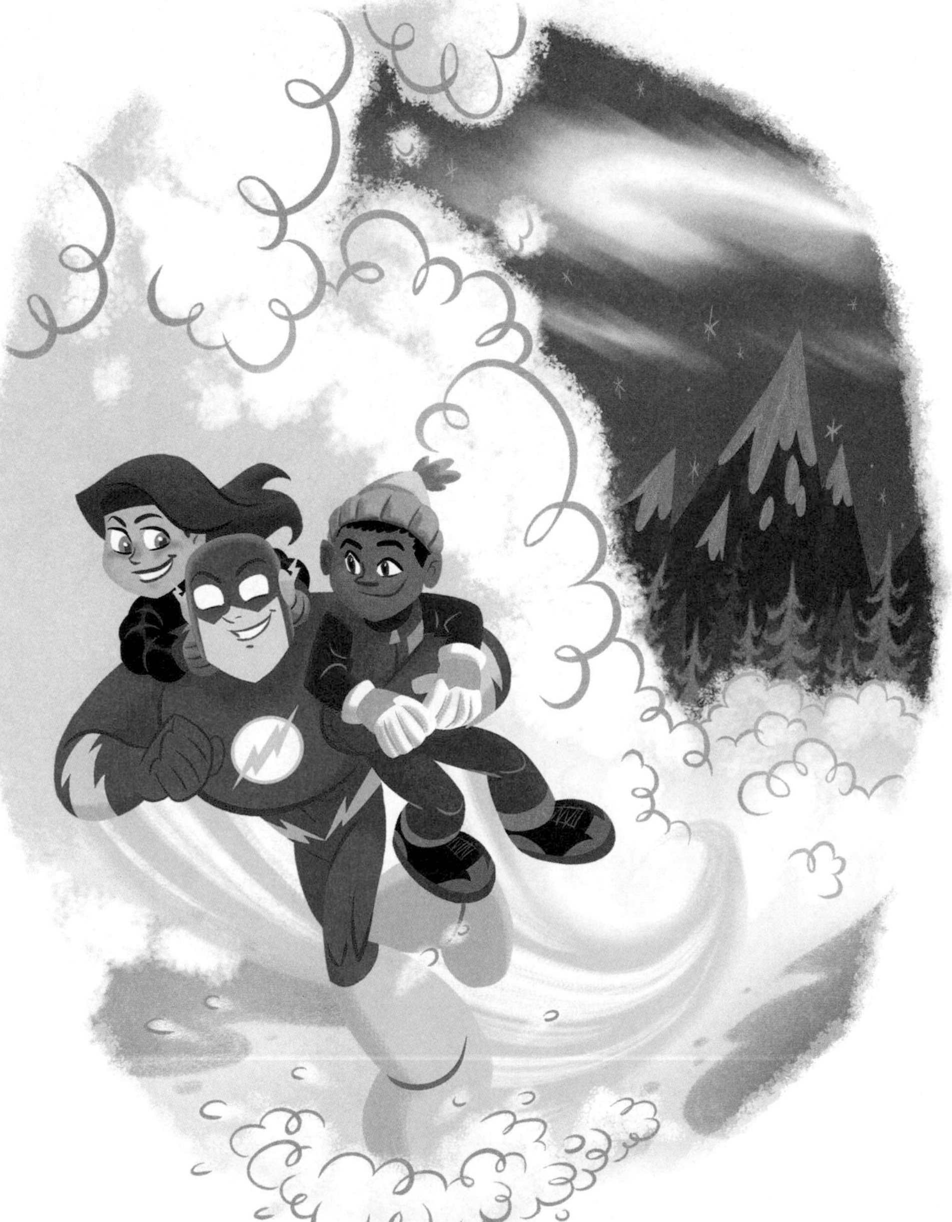

If you're in danger, don't blink. . . .

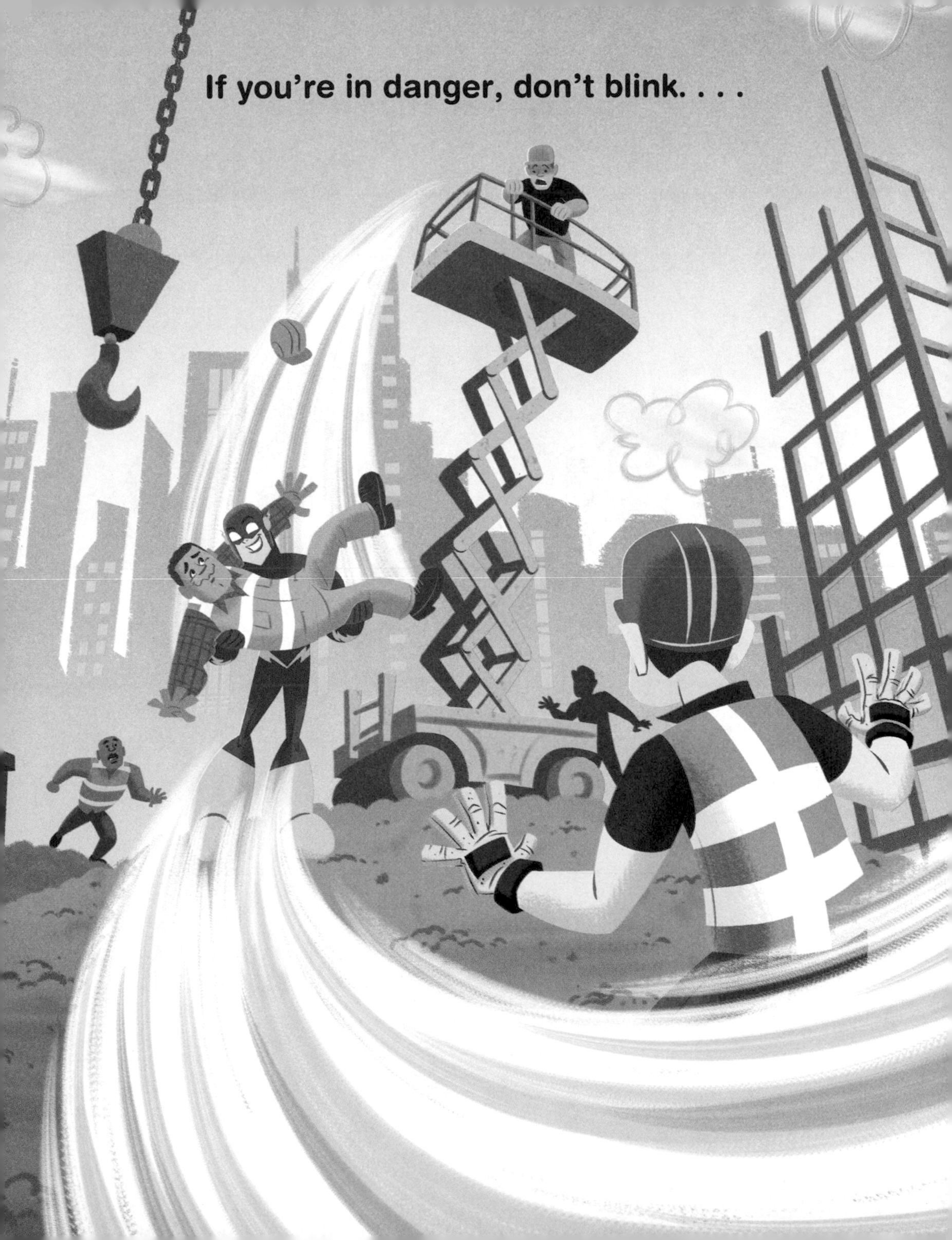

Here comes The Flash!

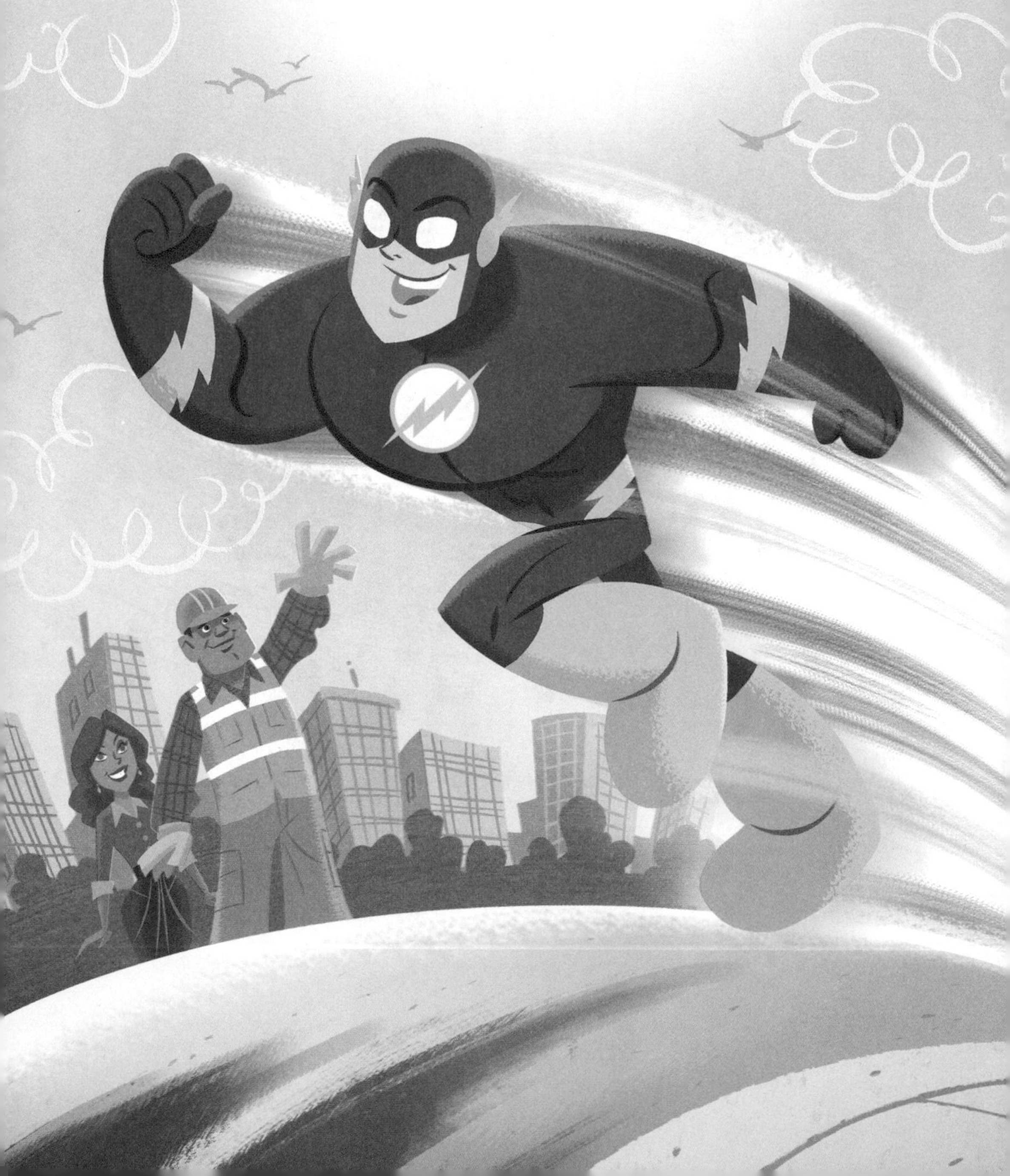